the la

If you char,
the librarian.

VOYAGES OF DISCOVERY

NEW HORIZONS IN HISTORY SERIES

The aim is to provide helpful background books in a variety of historical subjects of great appeal to young people in the 11 to 16 age range. The books draw extensively upon authentic sources for the maps and illustrations and are intended to sharpen interest and widen the area for research.

1. VOYAGES OF DISCOVERY *by H. J. M. Claessen*
2. HANNIBAL *by K. Sprey*
3. PILGRIMAGES *by C. W. Van Voorst Van Beest*

H. J. M. Claessen

VOYAGES
OF
DISCOVERY

LUTTERWORTH PRESS · GUILDFORD AND LONDON

First published in Great Britain 1974
ISBN 0 7188 1986 1
PUBLISHED IN HOLLAND © 1970 BY FIBULA – VAN DISHOECK N. V.
TRANSLATED INTO ENGLISH BY MARIAN POWELL
ENGLISH TRANSLATION © 1974 LUTTERWORTH PRESS

Printed in Great Britain by
Cox & Wyman Ltd.,
London, Fakenham and Reading

CONTENTS

INTRODUCTION

It started a very long time ago, this great adventure of exploring the earth. It was a slow and gradual process and many brave men took part in it. Their adventures have been described in bulky volumes and in ancient documents. Some, but by no means all, of these voyages will be mentioned in this book. To some of the explorers more attention will be paid than to others; some will merely be alluded to in passing; a few will be quoted. But it is not only the travellers who are of importance. Their ships and their methods of navigation play a part as well. Explorers who penetrated the interiors of Africa and America on foot had different problems. These, too, will be referred to. There is also the question why? What was the reason for all these voyages? What made the men set out?

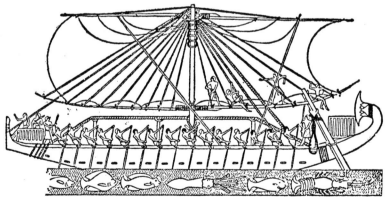

Painting of an Egyptian ship in one of the pyramids. It is in such a ship that Heno is believed to have travelled to the Land of Punt.

ANTIQUITY

From the pyramids to the Land of Punt

It all started a long time ago, long before the Christian era. At that time several tribes with a highly developed civilisation lived along the shores of the Mediterranean. It is from here that the first voyages of discovery were undertaken. Judging from the reports on some of these voyages which have been preserved, search for treasure was usually the chief motive. From ancient Egypt, for instance, we know the story of a voyage undertaken around 2000 B.C. by a nobleman called Heno, who set out on the instructions of Pharaoh Senusret. He was dispatched to the distant Land of Punt to fetch myrrh. From merchants' tales Heno had learned the approximate situation of this country, but their reports only mentioned the overland route, while he wanted to reach his goal by sea. As the Land of Punt lay in the region of what is now Somaliland, Heno first had to cross the desert for eight days until he

Carrying myrrh

The king and queen of the Land of Punt receiving the Egyptian ambassador

reached the shore of the Red Sea. There the Egyptians built a ship and then sailed southwards.

Little is known about the rest of the voyage, except that it was successful and that Heno was able to obtain the myrrh for his king.

In subsequent years the voyage was repeated several times, and in this way the Egyptians became familiar with the waters of the Red Sea and the Gulf of Aden.

During this time voyages were also undertaken in the Mediterranean. The Egyptians took part in these as well. However, their ships proved to be unsuitable for the open sea, as they could not withstand the high waves. The ships had been designed mainly for traffic on the Nile. As long as they kept well inshore – as on their voyages to the Land of Punt – the sailors were in little danger, but to cross the Mediterranean was a risky undertaking.

Merchants and settlers

The leading seafarers in the Mediterranean were not the Egyptians, but the inhabitants of Crete, a large, densely populated island. The ships of the Minoans, as the inhabitants of Crete were called around 1500 B.C., were suitable for sailing in open waters. The Minoans undertook voyages in all directions, with Knossos as their main home port. Archeological excavations, which produce a great many objects used by ancient peoples, have taught us that there have been Minoan traders in Cyprus, in Sicily and on the coast of Syria. They also traded with

9

Drawing of a ship on a vase found in Cyprus

Egypt. In this way all kinds of precious materials were distributed over a wide area: wood and fine fabrics from Syria, cattle from Asia Minor, sweetmeats and copper from Cyprus, perfumes from the Land of Punt and from Arabia, papyrus from Egypt.

Trading was no easy matter for seafarers in those days. Good harbours were few and far between. Sometimes the ships were merely beached. After their business had been completed the sailors would push the ship into the sea once more and row or sail on to the next place of call. Many trading voyages thus became voyages of discovery as well.

Crete's prosperity came to a sudden end when around 1400 B.C. the island was occupied by Greeks from Mycenae. This conquest gave the Mycenaeans a share in the Mediterranean trade. They in their turn added to the knowledge of land and sea. The Mycenaeans were a pugnacious people and often clashed with the inhabitants of the seashores. These clashes led to wars, and the account of one of these has been preserved. In the *Iliad* the Greek poet Homer describes how a number of 'heroes', under the command of Agamemnon, king of Mycenae, laid siege to the powerful fortified city of Troy on the Hellespont (the present-day Dardanelles). The siege lasted a long time. Gods intervened on both sides; all sorts of miracles

10

occurred, and finally the Greeks succeeded in taking the city by a ruse. They constructed a large wooden horse, in which a number of brave warriors hid one night. The Greeks then pretended to lift the siege. They withdrew, leaving the horse behind as a kind of gift. In triumph the Trojans pulled the horse into the city, as a symbol of victory, but that night the Greek soldiers crept out and opened the city gates from the inside. The Greeks, who had returned by stealth, entered and laid waste the city. According to scholars this happened around 1200 B.C.

Stories about voyages of discovery in antiquity are always connected with trade. Ships' captains were forever searching for new trading commodities and for new markets for their goods. Of these trading peoples the Phoenicians were to become the most important.

These people lived in the region which is now Syria and the Lebanon. Their chief cities were Tyre and Sidon. They were favourably situated: caravans brought precious

Minoan king and head priest

fabrics and jewellery from the interior to the coast and the products of Egypt, Crete and Greece were fetched from overseas.

In contrast to the boastful Mycenaeans, the Phoenicians talked little about their voyages. Fearing competition, they kept the details of their routes a secret, but nevertheless some particulars concerning their voyages and trade routes have survived. For instance, it is known that the Phoenicians searched for sources of tin and silver. These metals were of great value and were not found in the eastern Mediterranean. Ships therefore sailed to the west. They were strongly built freighters, with a flat bottom, sloping fore and aft, so that they could be easily beached. The holds were covered by a flat deck. Cargo was stowed both in the holds and on deck. A single mast carried a square sail and the rudder consisted of a very large oar, mounted aft on the right-hand side of the ship. Even now the right-hand side of a ship is called star ('steer') board. There were no cabins for the crew who had to eat and sleep on deck or among the cargo.

Near present-day Tunis the Phoenicians founded a colony, named Utica. From there they sailed further westwards. Finally a Phoenician captain ventured to pass the Pillars of Hercules, that is to say, he sailed through the Straits of Gibraltar and into the Atlantic. Tin and silver could not be far away. And indeed, the Phoenicians were on the right track. Shortly beyond the Pillars of Hercules they established another colony, from which the Spanish town Cadiz has grown. Silver was found in this region and tin could be bought cheaply. This came from England and was brought to southern Spain by an overland route. The actual tin mines were to remain out of reach of the Mediterranean peoples for many more centuries.

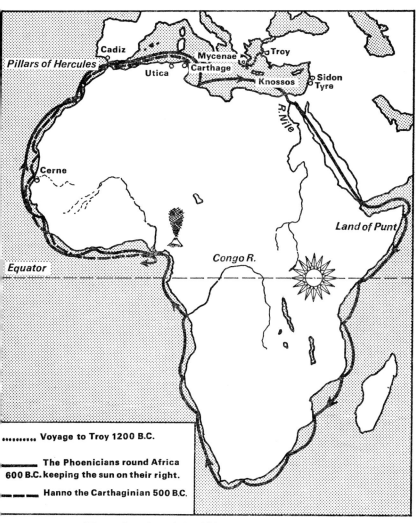

Cadiz

Pillars of Hercules

Utica

Mycenae
Carthage

Troy

Knossos

Sidon
Tyre

R. Nile

Cerne

Land of Punt

Congo R.

Equator

.... Voyage to Troy 1200 B.C.

———— The Phoenicians round Africa
600 B.C. keeping the sun on their right.

— — — Hanno the Carthaginian 500 B.C.

The exploration of the African coast in antiquity.

The capes of Africa

The Phoenicians not only went northwards, they also sailed in a southerly direction down the coast of N.W. Africa. The Greek historian Diodorus described what is said to have happened during one of these voyages.

In the middle of the ocean, opposite Africa, there lies a remarkably large island. It is no more than a few days' sailing from Africa. The Phoenicians, exploring the coast beyond the Pillars of Hercules, were blown by a strong wind from the African coast into the Atlantic. After having drifted around for some days, to their great amazement, they reached this island.

According to scholars, this must have been Madeira.

The most famous voyage ever made by Phoenician sailors was the one round Africa. This voyage was undertaken at the request of the Egyptian pharaoh Necho around 600 B.C. A short report has been preserved in the historical writings of the Greek Herodotus, which reads as follows:

Libya (that is, Africa) is clearly surrounded by sea, except where it borders on Asia. As far as we know this was first proved by the Egyptian king Necho. After having stopped the digging of a canal from the Nile to the Arabian Gulf,* he dispatched Phoenician sailors with the order to return to Egypt via the Pillars of Hercules and the Northern Sea. The Phoenicians set out from the Red Sea and sailed down the Southern Sea; each autumn they disembarked, sowed the land and waited for the harvest; after the harvest they continued their voyage until, in the third year, they passed between the Pillars of Hercules and once more reached Egypt. And they related something that I can hardly believe, though perhaps others can, namely, that whilst sailing round Libya they had had the sun on their right.

The remarkable feature of this report is that it is exactly the statement which Herodotus doubted that proves to present-day scholars that the story is true. For in sailing south from the Red Sea along the eastern seaboard of Africa and via its southern tip northwards along the west coast, the equator is crossed twice. The sun is near the equator all the year round and the sailors had therefore constantly seen it on their right.

The last of the great Phoenician explorers is known to us by name. This was Hanno, a nobleman from Carthage. This city had been founded long before as a Phoenician

* Probably what is now called the Gulf of Suez.

14

colony, but had soon become independent. Hanno had the story of his voyage depicted on the wall of one of the temples of Carthage. From this we have learned that around 500 B.C. he headed a large expedition to West Africa. The purpose of the voyage was to establish trading posts. The Carthaginians first sailed to the mouth of the river Senegal. Here they halted for some time to explore the surrounding area. It is probable that Hanno sailed up the river for a considerable distance. Finally he established a colony, called Cerne. Hanno and his men then continued down the coast. After having passed Cape Verde, the the voyage became exciting. Hanno himself relates:

When we landed on the smaller island we saw nothing but forests during the daytime. At night large fires were lit. We heard the sound of whistles, cymbals and drums and tremendous shouting. The soothsayers told me to leave the island. Being afraid, we left in a hurry. For four days on end we saw fires everywhere on land. In their midst was a fire larger than all the others, so large that it nearly reached the stars. By day we saw it was a mountain which we called the 'Chariot of the Gods'.

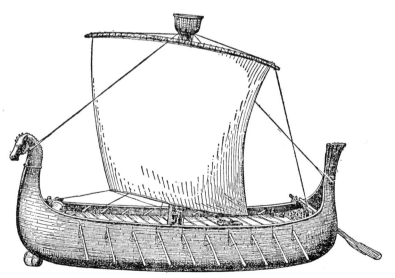

Phoenician warship from the 11th–8th century B.C.

Shortly afterwards the Carthaginians returned. Scholars believe that Hanno and his companions went south as far as Cameroon. In this region there is a volcano which, according to calculations, did in fact erupt around 500 B.C.

After the visit of the Carthaginians it was to be nearly 2000 years before white sailors once more ventured so far south along the coast of Africa.

Towards the misty north

In antiquity great expeditions were not confined to the seas only. As the various nations increased their trade – or their warfare – knowledge grew. Brave merchants, eager for profit, travelled to all parts of the world, thus adding to this knowledge. There were men who travelled merely to satisfy their curiosity. They just wanted to know what lay far away beyond the mountains or the desert. To this group belonged the scholars who set out to see and explore the wonders of the earth. The most important of these was Pytheas from Massilia, present-day Marseilles.

Around 350 B.C. he set out to seek the source of tin. It is probable that his expedition was paid for by merchants in Massilia, who were anxious to know the secret which the Phoenicians had been unable to learn.

Unfortunately only fragments have survived of Pytheas' account of his travels. From these we learn that he somehow managed to cross from Brittany to England. Here he visited the tin mines and watched the miners hacking the tin from the corridors, melting and purifying it and shaping it into blocks. These blocks were transported to Brittany in ships and from there were taken south by pack-animals. When he had learned all this, Pytheas continued his voyage. He sailed round England and discovered that it was an island. Several times he landed to meet the inhabitants and to study their customs.

16

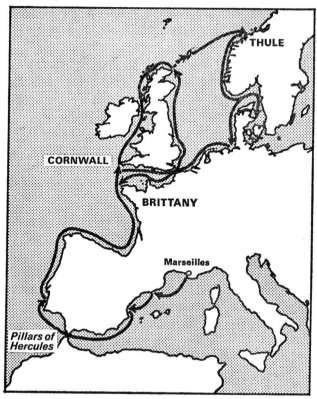

Voyage of Pytheas 350 B.C.

He went even further and visited the mysterious Land of Thule. Here he encountered ice and fog and drank beer made from barley and honey. From this information we may deduce that perhaps it was present-day Norway. Finally he visited the country which produced amber (petrified resin, much in demand for ornaments). Scholars have never been able to agree on the situation of this region. It is probable that it lay around the estuary of the river Elbe. Satisfied with all his discoveries, the traveller returned to Massilia.

Pytheas' voyage had few consequences. Sailors in antiquity did not feel at home in the cold Atlantic. Their interests lay in warmer seas.

The skippers of the empire

After the expeditions of Alexander the Great to the East, during which he established contact between Greeks and Persians, voyages in the Indian Ocean rapidly increased, both in number and in importance. In the time of the Roman emperors Augustus and Nero this area had become familiar. Roman skippers fetched incense from Arabia, ivory from East Africa, pepper and Chinese silk from India. They sailed across the Mediterranean to the Nile and from there via a canal to the Red Sea. After leaving the shores of the Red Sea the skippers made their way either to the coast of Africa or to Indian ports.

It is remarkable that hardly anything is known about the sailors who first made these voyages, although Roman writers eagerly recorded the tall stories which the voyagers related about foreign peoples and strange customs. When the sailors found that the stay-at-homes enjoyed their

In the Middle Ages it was thought that Pliny had seen monsters like these

Alexander the Great

stories, they invented more and more strange things. One of the Roman writers who recorded all this was Pliny. He tells us about people in Ethiopia who were said to have no mouth or nose, but a single opening in their head, through which they sucked in water and grains of corn by means of straws. In Pliny (c. 50 A.D.) we can also read that there were people in India whose feet were back to front, and people with dogs' heads. The strangest story is probably that of the Parasolopeds. These were supposed to be people with only one leg supported by a foot so large that they protected themselves from the hot sun by lying in the shade of this foot.

THE MIDDLE AGES

As long as Rome dominated the world as it was then known, sailors continued to make their voyages and tell their tales, but this changed when Rome's power came to an end.

The island Europe

A new era began and the story of the discovery of the earth continues.

The fall of the Roman Empire put an end to the age when the greater part of the known world was ruled by

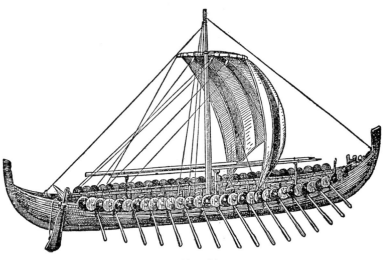

Viking ship

one nation. A time of wars and confusion began, during which much knowledge of the earth was lost. The European peoples who liked to think of themselves as the Romans' successors were threatened from all sides: in the south by the Saracens, Arabian people who were Mohammedans; in the east and north by 'heathens' – by this were meant people who were neither Christians nor Mohammedans.

Europeans did not travel a great deal in the early Middle Ages. If they travelled at all it was within their own familiar area. In the monasteries the ancient books of Roman writers were spelled out, from which it appeared that the world outside Europe was peopled with monsters. Sensible people who had read Pliny realised that it was safer to stay at home.

The only people who did not stay at home in the early Middle Ages were Irish missionaries. In the course of the voyages which they undertook in the eighth century to convert people to Christianity, they discovered Iceland. Shortly afterwards the Vikings arrived there. It is not known whether they, too, discovered the island themselves or whether they acted on rumours of its existence.

Forgotten explorers

These Vikings became the chief travellers of the early Middle Ages. The densely-populated, infertile coasts of Scandinavia forced them to put out to sea to build themselves an existence elsewhere. In their narrow ships, decorated with dragons and propelled by oars and sails, they marauded the surrounding waters. They soon extended their field of operations to the North Sea, where they plundered the coastal areas of England and France. Others entered the Baltic and traded with the inhabitants of Russia. A few Norsemen went as far as the Mediterranean. But the Vikings' most important discoveries were made in the west. From Iceland, where they had estab-

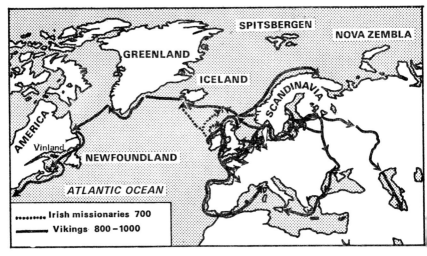

Voyages of the Vikings and of Irish missionaries

lished a large colony, they made distant voyages through storms and fog. On one of these voyages a new land suddenly loomed out of the mist: Greenland.

It was probably discovered by a ship which had been blown off course in a gale. Soon the Vikings visited it regularly and around the year 1000 they even established a colony in Greenland. It is believed that more than 3,000 people lived there. The colony was abandoned in the fifteenth century, but before this happened, the Vikings discovered America from here. The name of the man who found it is known: it was Bjarni Herjolfsson. He, too, was blown off course in a gale. He called the new land Vinland – the land where the vine grows. To Norsemen's ears it sounded like a fairy tale. On several occasions they tried to settle in the new land, but each time they clashed with the Skraelings – the monsters, as they called the Indians. They did not succeed in subduing these Skraelings. Ever more fighters appeared from the forests and finally the Norsemen had to give up their efforts. Nothing about their discoveries was heard in the other countries of Europe. People there were too busy with other matters to pay attention to the expeditions of the formidable Norsemen.

22

Wanderers over sand and sea

Nor was anything heard in Europe about the journeys of Arabian travellers. In Africa these were often journeys in the desert. They travelled through the hot, barren Sahara to the Sudan. These travellers were either traders in ivory, slaves or gold, or scholars who wanted to learn about foreign countries and peoples. Sometimes they were devout Mohammedans, anxious to spread their religion.

The writings of several Arabian travellers have been preserved. From these we learn that they not only travelled in North Africa, but also in large stretches of Asia. The most famous of these travellers was Ibn Batuta (1304–69), a lawyer from Tangier. His journey, which took over twenty-five years, first took him to Mecca, where he visited the tomb of Mohammed. He then went on to Baghdad and Constantinople, he visited the Crimea and after long wanderings reached Delhi in India, where he remained for a long time at the court of the Sultan.

Ibn Batuta's journey, 1325–49; 1350–52

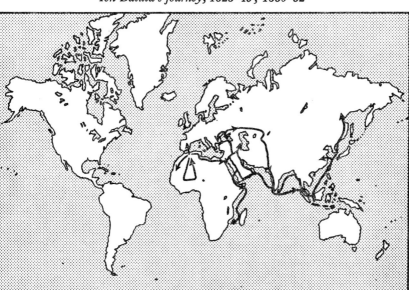

Copy of the map of Edrisi. Arabian view of the world, tenth century. To us the map is clearer seen upside down, when Spain, Greece and Arabia can be distinguished.

From here he visited Ceylon and Assam and finally reached China, where he was hospitably received at the emperor's court. He returned to Tangier via Sumatra, India and Syria. Later he went to West Africa and among other places visited Timbuktu. Altogether Ibn Batuta covered more than 75,000 kilometres – a distance equal to nearly twice the circumference of the earth. As a result of these travels Mohammedan scholars acquired a fair amount of knowledge about large parts of the earth.

The crusades of the eleventh and twelfth century for the first time put Europeans once more in contact with foreign countries and peoples. They had discovered that the Mohammedans were exceptionally strong and that the Crusaders were no match for them. They therefore sought help and are thought to have found it among the Mongolians.

These Mongolians (or Tartars) came from the steppes of Asia. Their armies had subjected large regions and had penetrated deep into Europe. The Mongolian horsemen on their shaggy little horses inspired dread in many rulers. It was only the death of the Khan in 1227 which had withheld them from a decisive attack on Europe. The Pope and the European rulers regarded these savage warriors as the only people who could bring down the mighty Mohammedans. To win them over to their plans, in the middle of the thirteenth century a number of embassies were sent out to the ruler of the Tartars. One of these ambassadors was the monk John de Plano Carpini, a stout old man who managed to cover the 4800 km. journey to the Khan's court in one hundred and six days. The court was situated in Karakorum, a few hundred kilometres south of Lake Baykal. The journey had been hard. The monk had had to travel thousands of kilometres through the steppes and the deserts of Asia. Snow-covered mountains needed to be crossed and he had often been short of food and drink. The court gave him a sympathetic reception and the Khan listened to his message with interest. A few days later Carpini was given a letter from the Khan to the Pope and set out on the long journey home. This was even harder than the way out, for meanwhile winter had arrived. Snowstorms howled over the plains and at night the biting cold often made it difficult to fall asleep. Exhausted the monk at last delivered his letter to the Pope. When he had recovered somewhat

25

he wrote a book about his travels and about the Mongolians, whom he had got to know well. For the first time Europeans received some idea about the countries and peoples of Asia.

A few years later another monk travelled to the Khan of the Mongolians. This time it was a Flemish monk called Willem van Rubroek, who went on the instruction of the French king. He, too, wrote a book about the Mongolians after his return from Karakorum.

Venetian travellers

The best known book about Asia was written in the prison of Pisa. Here a grey-haired merchant from Venice, who had been taken prisoner in a war between the two cities, dictated his story to his fellow-prisoner Rustichello: how as a young man he had left Venice with his father and his uncle to travel to the court of the Great Khan of the Mongolians, and what adventures had befallen them on their journey. The merchant's name was Marco Polo. The book contained so many remarkable things that, when Marco Polo lay on his death-bed, the Venetians said

Marco Polo

Kublai Khan, ruler of China at the time of Marco Polo

he should take back all the lies he had told. But Marco replied that he had only told half of what he had seen.

Marco Polo's journey had indeed been far and long enough to fill a big book with remarkable tales. The Polos had left in 1271 and the journey from Venice to Peking, where Kublai, the Great Khan, lived at that time, had taken three and a half years. The Polos travelled first through Turkey and Persia and then took the mountain road to the ancient city of Balkh. They then climbed the Pamir mountains, a range so high that it was sometimes called 'the roof of the world'. It took them twelve days to cross the plateau and in all that time they encountered neither man nor beast. After the Pamir mountains came endless steppes and deserts. Marco fell ill, and they had to wait a year before they could continue on their way, but finally the Venetians reached the court of Kublai Khan.

A warm welcome awaited them. The clever young Marco, in particular, pleased the ruler. Soon he entered the Khan's service and made long tours of inspection in the extensive Mongolian empire. He visited several cities in China, where he marvelled at all he saw. The Chinese knew the art of printing books and they used paper money. They had coal which burnt and asbestos which did not. Marco Polo described all these marvels in his book, and the Venetians did not believe him.

27

He visited Tibet and Burma and penetrated deep into Mongolia, but at last he wanted to go home. The Khan did not want to lose the services of this able fellow, but finally a good opportunity presented itself for his return. A Chinese princess was to marry a sultan in Persia and the Polos were entrusted with taking her there. They set off with a large fleet. In the course of the long voyage along the shores of Asia one ship after another was lost, so that after many months only a small company arrived in Persia. The sultan had died meanwhile and the princess married his son instead. The Polos continued on their way to Venice, their home town, which they had left twenty-four years earlier.

Now the way to the East lay open. European merchants began to trade in oriental wares: silk and ornaments, spices, weapons and many other things. Monks travelled to the East to spread the gospel of Christianity.

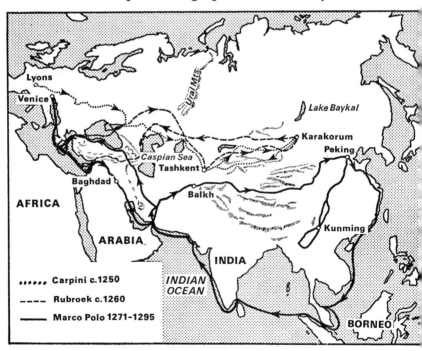

Expeditions in Asia

After Kublai Khan's death the Mongolians lost interest in the Europeans and their ideas. Some of the rulers were actually hostile to the people from the West. When in addition the power of the Mohammedans once more increased, Europeans ceased travelling to Asia. New ways had to be found to reach the souls of the 'heathens', as well as the precious spices.

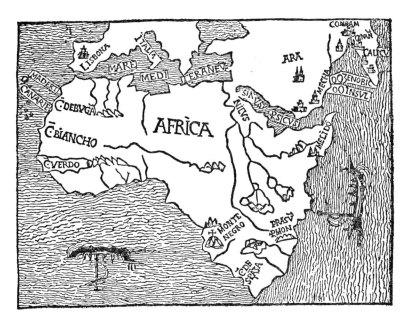

Portuguese map of 1508. C. DEBVGA = Cape Bojador

THE GREAT ERA

Crusades, caravels and cloves

In the East the Mohammedans had become more power-ful; in the West, on the other hand, their might decreased. For centuries the Spaniards and Portuguese had waged war against the Moors (as the Mohammedans were called there) and it looked as if they were to get the upper hand. The Portuguese actually went so far as to fight the Mohammedans in North Africa. Some scholars call this the last crusade.

It was these campaigns which aroused interest in Africa among the Portuguese. Africa – was not this where gold and pepper came from? Perhaps they could kill two birds with one stone: fight the Moors and at the same time initiate a profitable trade . . . It is difficult to establish which of these two motives had most attraction for the Portuguese. Pepper was of great importance to people in Europe. It was used to give flavour to their food. There were no refrigerators or tinned foods in those days. The only method by which food could be preserved was by salting it – but this did not improve the taste. Cooks therefore tried to improve the flavour by using strong spices. Only very rich people could afford this kind of food, for pepper was expensive. The pepper trade yielded high profits.

When the Moors proved to be stronger than the Portuguese had thought, a further reason arose for continuing the exploration of the African coast. It was rumoured that far away, in the interior of Africa, there lived a Christian people, ruled by the priest-king John. The Portuguese wanted to find him and try to turn him into an ally against the Sultan. And moreover . . . moreover there was the strong rumour that somewhere, beyond Africa – it was not known how and where – lay the mysterious land of India, the country from which nearly all spices came. Up to that time cinnamon and cloves could be bought only from the Venetians, who in turn bought them from Mohammedan traders. Prices were high, and the Portuguese began to dream of the possibility of finding the way to India and of acquiring at least part of this trade.

Of course individual travellers were not inspired by all these motives at once. As a rule one of them prevailed, but there were men who took a wider view. One of these men was Dom Enrique – or Prince Henry – nicknamed the Navigator. Between 1420 and 1460 he dispatched his captains to explore the coast of Africa in their caravels, as their ships were called. The information they brought back was carefully recorded and studied. In this way a sort of school for sailors developed in Lisbon, where all existing knowledge of Africa was gathered.

Mile after mile the ships explored the unknown shores. The voyage of Hanno the Carthaginian had been forgotten, as had been those of the Phoenicians of the time of Pharaoh Necho. Everything was new to the Portuguese and the captains were afraid of the foreign shore and the unknown dangers. Had not Pliny, the Roman author, written tales of giants who upset ships, of currents which drove the ships on to dangerous rocks and of dragons who threatened the lives of seamen? One cannot but admire the courage of these sailors, who, although believing in dragons and giants, nevertheless obeyed their master in Lisbon and sailed on. Fortunately the travellers soon realised that these dangerous creatures must live a long way away, for however distant their voyages, they never encountered them.

In 1434 the caravels passed Cape Bojador, in 1444 they

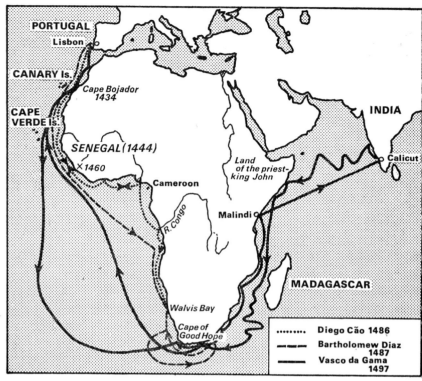

Round Africa to India

reached the Senegal River and in 1460 they sighted the
mountains of Sierra Leone. That year Henry the Navigator died and the Portuguese advances were halted for
some years.

But soon a new leader came to the fore, namely the
merchant Fernando Gomez, and the captains in his service
reached Cameroon.

Particularly great exploits were achieved during the
reign of King John II. The brave captain Diego Cão was
the first to reach the estuary of the Congo River. He made
friends with the ruling negro king and sailed a long way
up the river. His second voyage, in 1486, took him even
further south, as far as Walvis Bay in present-day South-
West Africa.

32

Diego Cão discovered how difficult it was to take sufficient food and drinking water for long voyages in the small caravels. His successor, Bartholomew Diaz, therefore took along a special supply ship. He went even further south than Cão and one day was blown offshore by a strong gale. When after a few days the wind abated, the Portuguese tried to reach land again by sailing east. Although they kept a sharp lookout, they did not see the expected coast and Diaz therefore decided to turn north. That way he must get somewhere. And indeed, land came in sight and the captain realised that he must have passed the southernmost point of Africa in the gale. He therefore called this point the Cape of Storms. He wanted to continue to explore the route to India, but his sailors lacked courage. They had been away from home for a long time and the food supplies were getting low. They persuaded Bartholomew Diaz to return to Portugal.

The southern tip of Africa had been reached and it was hoped that long-cherished dreams would now be realised. King John therefore changed the name of the Cape of Storms into Cape of Good Hope.

His successor, King Manuel, entrusted the command of the decisive expedition to Vasco da Gama, who set off in 1497 with four specially built ships. After a prosperous voyage the Cape of Good Hope was reached, but now trouble began. The ships slowly crept up the east coast of Africa with both wind and current against them. To their surprise the Portuguese discovered that the inhabitants of these shores were not 'savages' like the people they had found on Africa's other coast. They found large seaports, ruled by proud sultans, who looked at the gifts they were offered with contempt.

In one of these ports the Portuguese at last heard news of the priest-king John. A member of the crew, Alvaro Velho related it as follows in his journal:

They told us that the priest John ruled not far from here. That he reigned over numerous cities on the coast, whose inhabitants were merchants owning many ships. The capital of priest John's realm lay inland and could be reached only by camel. This information and much besides made us cheer for happiness and we prayed to God that we might stay in good health so that we might achieve what we so intensely wanted.

Finally they found a pilot who led them across the Indian Ocean to the port of Calicut. But here a disappointment awaited the Portuguese. The Mohammedan merchants who lived there were not at all pleased that the Christians from the West had found the way to India. For that is where they were: in India. They had achieved the goal for which sacrifices had been made for so many years.

But they did not enjoy their stay in Calicut. The local merchants did everything in their power to make life difficult for them. For instance, they refused to supply them with food and tried to prevent the Portuguese from

Vasco da Gama

trading. Nevertheless Vasco da Gama finally succeeded in loading a cargo of spices and the return voyage began.

On the way back the Portuguese suffered a great deal from a disease which until then had hardly ever occurred, namely scurvy. The disease is caused by lack of fresh vegetables and meat; its symptoms are blisters in the mouth. Unless the patients receive proper food they die. It was the first time that sailors had encountered this dangerous illness on a large scale. Up till then they had sailed close to the coast, so that they could repeatedly replenish their scanty stores with fresh food. Out in the open sea this was, of course, not possible. The scurvy had disastrous consequences: more than half the crew died.

Calicut

As a result of the voyage, the way to the priest-king John had been found, but when the Portuguese king's ambassadors visited him at his court in Ethiopia, he proved by no means to be the powerful ally they had hoped to find. Nevertheless, Portugal rejoiced: at least trade with India could begin.

India – yes or no?

While the Portuguese caravels sailed along the shores of Africa, the Spaniards were engaged on their own soil in a long war against the Moors. The war came to an end in 1492 when Granada, the Moorish capital, fell to the Spanish. An unknown seaman from Genoa took the opportunity to extract money from the Spanish king to finance an expedition to Asia. On 3 August 1492, the seaman set off from the small port of Palos and steered his three small ships westward into the Atlantic. This voyage was to make him famous. He was Christoforo Colombo – whom we call Christopher Columbus – the discoverer of America.

Columbus' ships were little more than nutshells and their equipment was primitive. Food had to be cooked on deck over an open fire laid on a layer of sand. A small screen

The type of ship in which Columbus discovered America

Christopher Columbus

protected the fire from the wind. The food was monotonous and coarse: dried peas, beans, salted meat and ship's biscuits. Drinking water was carried in wooden barrels and most of it went bad in the course of the voyage. Only the captain had a cabin with a bunk. The rest of the crew slept in their clothes wherever they could find a place to lie down.

The voyage went smoothly – so smoothly that the sailors were frightened. The weather was too good. Was it never going to rain, so that they could replenish their supply of drinking water? The wind continued to blow from the same direction: towards the west. Would they ever be able to turn back? Tension on board mounted. Finally the crew threatened mutiny. Columbus, who felt that they were approaching land, persuaded the men to sail on for three more days. If by then they had not reached land they would turn back. But fortunately this did not happen. On 12 October 1492 the *Pinta*'s lookout

Indians smoking tobacco

sighted land. It proved to be one of the islands which we now call the Bahamas. Dressed in his best uniform, Columbus went ashore and named the island San Salvador. Thinking he had reached India, he called the new-found territories the West Indies and the inhabitants Indians. This is still the name by which the native inhabitants of America are known, but it is founded on a mistake by Columbus.

After a short stay the Spaniards continued on their way, believing they were near the coast of Asia. A few days later they sighted a large island, Cuba. Columbus thought he had reached Japan. He dispatched envoys into the interior, led by Luis de Torres, who spoke Hebrew and Arabic, and by Rodrigo de Xeres who had once visited an African chief and was therefore regarded as an expert in associating with foreign rulers. Naturally the ambassadors did not find the emperor of Japan, but they came back with the report that they had seen men 'eating smoke'. This was the first time that Europeans had seen tobacco being smoked.

After some further explorations, Columbus returned to Spain where he reported on his expedition to the king and queen, making it appear as if a great deal of gold was to be found in the territories he had discovered. This was to make his employers anxious to take possession of the new land.

The brave seaman was covered with honours and fame. He was appointed Admiral of the Ocean, Viceroy and Governor of the new territories.

A few months later he sailed out once more, again to 'Asia', which he believed he had so nearly reached. Columbus died in this belief, but some of his contemporaries realised that it was not Asia, but a New World which Columbus had found. One of the first to give expression to this idea was Amerigo Vespucci, a Florentine merchant who had made several voyages along the shores of the newly discovered land. That is why his name was given to the continent, which in future was to be called America.

Amerigo Vespucci

Knights and robbers

Once the Spaniards realised that a New World had been discovered, all kinds of enterprising men made for the area. They were people who shrank from nothing and nobody, and who were determined to acquire fame and riches in the land overseas. Sword in hand they set out. These men were called the Conquistadores – the conquerors. They were soldiers as well as merchants, but at the same time they were robbers and explorers. Within a short space of time they were to give Spain a world empire. Some of the Conquistadores had a further motive for going to America. They wanted to convert the 'heathen' in the distant lands to Christianity – if necessary by force of arms.

The peaceful Indian tribes of the coastal areas were no match for these bands of robbers. Within a short time thousands of the native inhabitants of the New World were killed or driven into the interior, while thousands of others were forced into slavery by the Spaniards, who rapidly penetrated the country.

As early as 1513, Vasco Nuñez de Balbao, who, in spite of his grand name was somewhat of a robber-chief, drove his Indian guides and porters across the mountains of Central America, until at last they halted on the shore of an unknown sea. The Pacific Ocean had been discovered and Balbao took possession of it on behalf of Spain by riding his horse into the water, where he made the sign of the cross with his sword.

Another Conquistador, perhaps the most important of them all, was Hernando Cortez. In 1519 he entered the mighty Aztec kingdom with a few hundred soldiers. These Aztecs differed greatly from the Indians whom the Spaniards had so far encountered. They were well organised in a large kingdom with strongly walled cities. They were ruled by a powerful king and in their temples regularly made human sacrifices to the gods. Cortez might have lost the battle against the large, well-armed and martial Aztec armies, but the Indians did not fight. They had been forbidden to do so by their king, Montezuma, who had heard ancient tales of a god who had departed but had promised to return one day. Perhaps this mysterious stranger was the Godhead . . .

After a successful expedition, Cortez reached Tenochtitlan, the capital of the kingdom. One of his travel companions, Bernal Diaz, who later wrote a book about his adventures in America, described it as follows:

What we saw was so strange that we could hardly tell whether it was real or whether we were dreaming. Large cities lay along the shores of the lake and on the islands. The lake was covered with canoes. In many places the road crossed bridges and in

Cortez with his interpreter Doña Marina talking to the Indians. Print from a Mexican book.

front of us lay Mexico (i.e. Tenochtitlan). There were only four hundred of us and we remembered the warnings of people from other tribes: that we should take care not to enter the city, as we would be killed as soon as we did so. Nevertheless we went on.

The Spaniards were received hospitably and ceremoniously. They were housed in a palace and everybody was very kind to them. But soon the difficulties began. Cortez' only thought was how to conquer this rich land and make it into a Spanish colony. Montezuma tried to find out whether or not the stranger was the expected god. Soon clashes occurred. Cortez took Montezuma prisoner and the king, believing it was the will of the gods, resigned himself to his fate. But the other Aztec leaders did not see it this way and attacked the Spaniards. After fierce fighting Cortez finally gained victory. The Aztec kingdom ceased to exist and became a Spanish colony.

Cortez' expedition was very similar to one undertaken by the Pizarro brothers in 1532 to the mysterious 'Golden Land' in South America. They too reached a rich and powerful empire: that of the Incas. The Pizarros crossed the Andes Mountains by well-made roads, and by treachery succeeded in capturing the Inca ruler Atahualpa, who had then just come to power. When the king saw how eagerly the Spaniards gathered gold, he offered to ransom himself. Pizarro demanded that the great hall of the palace should be filled with gold. This was to be the largest ransom ever paid. The messengers of the Sapa Inca (the

Cortez' signature

The Spanish advance in Mexico, seen through Indian eyes

king) ran out to all parts of the country and after a few weeks the gold began to stream in – enough to fill the hall ... But the Spaniards did not release the king. They were afraid that he would assemble his armies to fight them. They decided to kill Atahualpa. A reason was easily found: he was falsely accused of treason and was condemned to death.

Here too, the Conquistadores soon succeeded in subjecting the people, robbed of its leaders. Here too, as in Mexico, a flourishing native civilisation was destroyed by European arms.

From this colony further conquests were made. On one such expedition Francisco de Orellana in 1542 discovered the Amazon.

This soldier had been sent out with a few men to find food for a Spanish army which was roaming the forests at the foot of the Andes. In a number of boats they went downstream on a small river, but after some time they found that the strong current would prevent them from going back. They therefore decided to go on, thinking they would find the coast from where they could go back to their army. The plan turned out very differently. The voyage down river lasted eight months and the narrow stream became wider and wider. Its course led through the humid, sultry jungle of South America and the Spaniards repeatedly had to fight Indians on the banks of

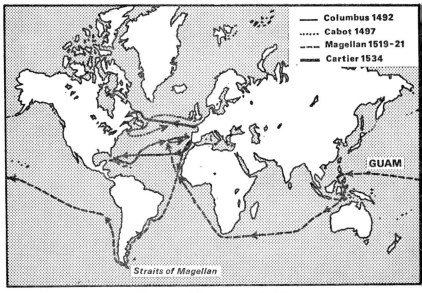

Voyages of discovery to the West

the river. When at last they reached the coast it was that of the Atlantic. They had crossed an entire continent, from west to east, by river. They had conquered the largest river in the world – the Amazon had been explored.

The first voyage round the world

Vasco da Gama had opened the way to the East, to India. Columbus had gone west and had reached America. It was only a question of time before someone would connect the two discoveries. In 1519 the Portuguese sailor Ferdinand Magellan departed in the service of Spain for his voyage round the world. Five small ships with a total crew of two hundred and eighty sailed out. Only one ship with thirty-one men was to return home – but the first voyage round the world had been accomplished! From the very beginning there had been difficulties. The Spanish sailors did not want to be commanded by a

Portuguese; it took five months to reach the southernmost point of South America and the food they carried turned out to be of bad quality. Only Magellan's iron will made the men go on. The voyage through the Straits of Magellan took thirty-eight days. For thirty-eight days the men and their ships struggled against gales and currents, constantly threatened by rocks and reefs. One ship was lost, a second fled back to the safe Atlantic, but Magellan persevered until at last the open waters of the Pacific lay before him.

The fleet first sailed a long way up the west coast of South America; then the great crossing began. Unfortunately the course which Magellan set meant that he did not encounter a single island of any importance on the long voyage. For ninety-six endless days the voyage continued. Food supplies diminished daily and the drinking water continually deteriorated. Death became a travelling companion. Soon the first sailors began to show symptoms of scurvy and shortly afterwards most of the men were ill. The few who were not affected by the disease

Magellan's compass

Magellan's map, 1586. From the journal of a later world traveller

were weakened by hunger and thirst. In the end they ate
and drank whatever they could lay their hands on. One of
the crew, a man called Pigafetta, wrote in his journal:

> We ate ship's biscuits reduced to crumbs and full of vermin. We
> drank water that had turned yellow and stank. We ate the strips
> of ox-hide round the yard-arms; we even ate sawdust. Rats
> were a delicacy for which a lot of money was paid.

At last the exhausted members of the expedition
reached the island of Guam, where they could recover
somewhat. Then Magellan and his men continued their
voyage. In the Philippines a new blow befell the expedition. In the course of an insignificant fight with the native
inhabitants, Magellan was killed. The hundred and fifteen
surviving members of the crew decided to leave the worst
of the three ships behind and continued in the two others
to the Molucca Islands, where they bought spices. Here
the two ships separated. One of them was shortly afterwards seized by the Portuguese who in those days ruled
in Indonesia; the crew was imprisoned. Only four of
them reached home many years later. The other ship at
last came back to Spain via the Cape of Good Hope. The
voyage round the world had lasted over three years.

46

THE ENGLISH, THE FRENCH AND THE DUTCH

To the Eskimos and the Indians

Of course it was not only the Spanish and the Portuguese who played a part in the history of voyages of discovery. In the same period sailors from other countries made similar voyages. Although their expeditions were not as great as those of Columbus and Magellan, they nevertheless form part of the story.

First of all we must mention the Cabots, father and son. Around the year 1500 they were instructed by the English king Henry VII to sail westwards to reach Asia. It had become known that a certain Columbus had arrived in the West Indies by sailing in a westerly direction. The two Cabots set off and soon found themselves in unknown territory – present-day Canada. At first they thought they were in northern Asia, but it soon became clear that they,

Eskimos. From the travel journal of Martin Frobisher

arrived in the New World, America. The
.1en then made several attempts to sail past the
n coast of the new continent in order to reach
Jut the barren climate and the cold, frozen polar
.nade it impossible. Well known are the voyages of
tne Frenchmen Cartier who in 1534 discovered the St.
Lawrence River; of the scholarly seaman Martin Frobisher,
who penetrated so deeply into the polar regions that he
encountered Eskimos; of John Davis, who got no further
than Greenland; and of William Baffins, who in 1615
reached the far end of the Hudson Bay. They were all
capable seamen, but none of them succeeded in reaching
Asia.

Other travellers penetrated deep into America. The
French, especially, went a long way into the interior. In
1608 Samuel Champlain reached the Great Lakes via the
St. Lawrence and thus laid the foundations for a French
colony in Canada. Setting out from this colony, Robert
Cavelier La Salle in 1682 explored the Mississippi. He
and his companions went all the way down this river in
Indian canoes, until they reached the Gulf of Mexico.

Beyond the ice must be India

Portugal was only a small country and there were not
enough men who wanted to go to sea. It was for this
reason that foreigners often took part in the voyages by
caravel to the spice islands of India. The trade in cloves
and nutmeg became more and more important – so much
so, that the struggle against the Mohammedans faded into
the background. Immense fortunes were made as well as
lost in the India trade. Of course other countries also
wanted to attempt the adventure, but the Portuguese tried
to keep the details of their route a secret and boasted
greatly of their power at sea.

One of the foreigners in Portuguese service used his
eyes and ears to good effect and noticed that the power of

48

the Portuguese was not really so great. He was called Jan Huyghen van Linschoten, a young man from Enkhuizen in Holland, who had set out from home at an early age. 'Day and night I long to visit foreign countries. That way one has something to talk about in one's old age', he once wrote in a letter to his mother. For over seven years he roamed the Portuguese territories in south-east Asia. He described his experiences in a book which made a great impression on the Dutch. If the Portuguese were really so weak as this Van Linschoten wrote, one might venture to go to India and China oneself! Rich merchants collected a great deal of money and experienced seamen were signed on for an exploratory voyage.

In those days it was still thought that it would be possible to reach the spice islands by the northern route. This way might be shorter and possibly less dangerous than the voyage round Africa.

In 1595 two ships left Amsterdam for a polar expedition. One was commanded by Jan Corneliszoon van de Rijp, the other by Jacob van Heemskerck, whose helmsman was Willem Barents. The first land they discovered was Spitsbergen, where they saw geese and reindeer. When they continued on their way a difference of opinion arose on the course to be followed. It was decided that the two ships should separate. Barents and Heemskerck went eastwards, De Rijp westwards.

The expedition of Barents and Van Heemskerck has become famous. After a long voyage in the Arctic they reached the large island of Nova Zembla. They believed that the worst was behind them, for in the distance they sighted open water; but they were much mistaken. They could not reach the water, for the ice was too thick; nor could they go back, for the ice had closed in behind them. Matters were to become even worse. Ice-floes began to press against the ship and a strong gale drove it on to the ice. The hull began to creak and the crew realised that the ship was lost. All kinds of stores were rapidly taken across the ice to the land and part of the crew was ordered to

'The House of Safety'

build a house. It was ready just in time, before the polar winter reached its full severity. The crew called it 'Behouden Huys' ('The House of Safety'). The winter spent in Nova Zembla was not easily forgotten. The men were repeatedly threatened by polar bears. Once a snow-plough, commanded by Van Heemskerck, which had gone to the ship, was attacked by three bears at once. The only weapons available were two lances with which the men tried to fend off the animals. The adventure had a happy ending, for the polar bears at last ran off. On another occasion it was only possible to keep the animals off by throwing pieces of burning wood at them.

When the winter became even more severe, the men remained indoors. They suffered greatly from the cold, although they used hot bricks to warm their feet. One of the Dutchmen, Gerrit de Veer, wrote in his journal:

It was so cold that, when we stretched out our feet to the fire, our socks burned before we could feel the warmth. We had to darn our socks repeatedly. In fact, if we had not smelled the

Bear hunt in Nova Zembla

scorching, our socks would have burned altogether without our feeling the heat.

Slowly the barren winter passed. For weeks on end the men could not leave the house because of the mountain of snow which blocked the door. They could only go out occasionally for short periods by way of the chimney.

Stores of food gave out and fuel supplies were also getting low. But at last the cold began to lessen slightly. By now it was April. Here and there patches of open water could be seen. Van Heemskerck was still hopeful that the ship might be usable when it became free from the ice, so that they could go home in it. But unfortunately his hopes were not realised and finally he had to give the order to make the ship's boats ready. On 14 June 1596 the Dutchmen set out on their return voyage. In their open rowing boats they cautiously made their way through the ice-floes, until they reached land. Some of the men, including Willem Barents, died of exhaustion. At last the survivors reached the peninsula of Kola, where they were given food and drink by the Russians who lived there. Rested and restored they continued on their way until they were picked up by a Dutch ship which strangely enough was captained by their former travelling companion De Rijp. He had returned to his fatherland after an unsuccessful attempt to find a way through in the west, and now found himself for the second time in the Arctic.

Round the Cape of Good Hope and Cape Horn

The way 'round the north' had proved to be impossible and so the Dutch were forced to go 'round the south'.

A fleet under the command of Cornelis de Houtman and Pieter Keyser set out for India and reached Java after a difficult voyage. The travellers had followed the route of the Portuguese and like them had suffered greatly from scurvy. In the spring of 1597 the survivors returned to Amsterdam: only ninety of the two hundred and ninety crew members saw their fatherland again. But this did not deter the Dutch. Other fleets soon set out and within a few years the spice market had shifted from Portuguese Lisbon to Dutch Amsterdam.

In 1652 Jan van Riebeeck, on the instructions of the United East India Company, founded the 'Cape Colony'

near the Cape of Good Hope. It was intended to be a port of call, where the East-Indiamen could take on food and drinking water. This greatly improved the health of the seamen.

This United East India Company was an association formed by the leaders of the various long distance trading companies at the insistance of Van Oldenbarnevelt. The association had the monopoly of trading with South East Asia. Its governing body dealt rigorously with outsiders who tried to circumvent the rules of the Company, as Jacob le Maire and Willem Schouten discovered to their cost.

These men had left the Dutch port of Hoorn in 1615 in order to seek new trading grounds in the Far East without violating the rights of the United East India Company. In particular they had the mysterious Southern Continent in mind. For in those days scholars believed that there must be a large unknown continent in the southern Pacific.

The two seamen found a new route round the southern-most part of South America, which they called Cape Horn after their home town, and then began their search for the Southern Continent. But however hard they tried, they did not find it. They only discovered a number of small islands where coco-palms grew and where the inhabitants watched the strange ships in amazement. Later they found some slightly larger islands, where they stayed a few days to take in food and water. These were some of the Tonga Islands. Finally they arrived in the regions monopolised by the East India Company. In Java the travellers received a serious blow. The Governor-General, Jan Pieterszoon Coen, seized their ships and imprisoned the crew. On the return journey Le Maire died, a prisoner of the United East India Company.

Exploration on behalf of merchants

The attention of the United East India Company had now been drawn to the Southern Continent. There had been earlier tales of skippers who, blown off course, had found an unknown coast south of Java. One of them, Willem Jansz, had sailed a long way down this coast in his ship

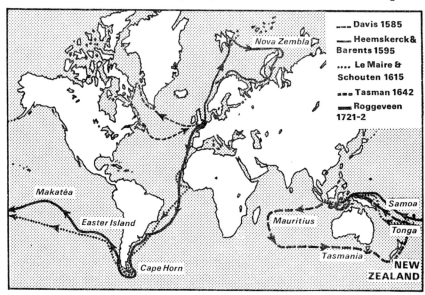

There is more than one route to India. . . .

Het Duyfke. This was sufficient reason for the leaders of the U.E.I.C. to have the matter thoroughly investigated. Abel Tasman, a seaman from Groningen, was entrusted with the command of the expedition and in 1642 the ships departed. Their first destination was the island of Mauritius. From there the ships turned some way south and began their search for the unknown continent. They set a constant easterly course and thus arrived at the southern coast of Australia. A number of landings in the deserts of this continent soon convinced the captain that there was little to be found here. Since the ships kept well away from the coast, it was not noticed that the area which Tasman regarded as the southern point of Australia was, in fact an island. This island was subsequently called Tasmania after its discoverer. After having passed it, the ships continued further eastwards and after a few days reached another large island: New Zealand. The inhabitants, the Maoris, were not in the least impressed by the strangers in their large ships. On the contrary, their canoes set out in large numbers and heavy fighting occurred. Having been instructed to find trading areas, Tasman left this inhospitable region as soon as he could.

Once more on the high seas, the leaders of the expedition decided to search for the Tonga Islands discovered by Schouten and Le Maire. After a few days' sailing they were sighted. Here they were much more hospitably received and the Dutchmen replenished their diminished stores with meat, coconuts and water. Hugging the shores of New Guinea, Tasman returned to Batavia. The gentlemen of the Company were disappointed. The new regions offered no opportunities for trading.

THE EIGHTEENTH CENTURY

The search for the Southern Continent

Ships became bigger. They carried more cargo and more sail. They were also more solidly built.

Shipbuilders were always attempting to improve the hull, the masts and the rigging. The nutshells in which Columbus and Magellan had sailed had been replaced by larger and stronger ships, consisting of several decks. Down in the hull they carried heavy stones to maintain the ship's balance. Next came a hold where food supplies and water barrels were stored, as well as part of the trading cargo. Above this came the artillery deck, where cannons were mounted. In those days no ship would set out without sufficient armament, and the sailors had to be able not only to handle the sails, but also the guns. Part of the cargo was stowed here as well. The high fore-part of the ship was called the forecastle, and here the crew lived as best they might. The part behind the main mast was also built up. Here were the officers' cabins, the day cabin and the chartroom. This was also where the helmsman stood. The rear end of the ship was the highest part of all, the poop. Here the captain or his mate stood when determining the ship's position. To do so they had to measure the height of the sun at certain times of the day by means of the Jacob's staff.

A Jacob's staff was a ruler with a sliding cross-piece. The staff was held at eye-level and the cross-piece was slid along it until one end touched the horizon and the other the sun. The altitude of the sun could then be read on the staff.

Jacob's staff

To ascertain their speed, seamen used a log. This was a block of wood which was thrown into the water, attached to a cord knotted at intervals. The number of knots sliding through the observer's hand within a certain length of time was counted and the number of 'knots' per hour was the speed of the ship.

To measure time a sand-glass was used. The disadvantage of these hour-glasses is that they have to be turned over regularly. On busy days this was sometimes forgotten, so that the exact time was often a matter of guess-work.

No effective means to combat scurvy had yet been found. It was realised that the disease was due to lack of fresh food, but there was as yet no method to preserve foodstuffs.

That is how matters stood at the beginning of the

eighteenth century. At that time we find another Dutch-
man, the lawyer Jacob Roggeveen, who in 1721 and 1722
in his turn searched for the mysterious Southern Continent. Roggeveen's voyage in many ways resembled that of
Le Maire and Schouten a century earlier. Again the crew
suffered from scurvy and lack of food. Again the travellers
were taken prisoner and their ships seized by the leaders
of the United East India Company when at last they
reached Batavia. The only result of this voyage, undertaken with such high hopes, was the discovery on Easter
Day, 1722, of a large island – ever since called Easter
Island – and of the Samoa Islands. The Southern Continent remained hidden in the wide expanse of the great
ocean.

The conquest of the ocean

Around the middle of the eightcenth century various
scholars in England pressed for further exploration of the
Pacific. They believed that they would be able to prevent
the greatly-feared scurvy. Research into this disease had

*Jacob Roggeveen and his men looking at the large stone images on
Easter Island*

been carried out chiefly by a certain Dr. Lind. He had come to the conclusion that the disease was much more prevalent in overcrowded, dirty ships than in less crowded, properly cleaned vessels and also that drinking lemon juice was a good preventative against the illness. James Cook was to put these conclusions to the test.

The appointment of James Cook as commander of the great English expedition to the Pacific crowned a remarkable career, which had started in 1740 when the young James had been taken on as a junior assistant in an untidy ship-chandler's shop in a small fishing port. From here he could see and smell the sea, but that might have been all if one day skipper John Walker had not asked him to become ship's boy on his collier, the *Freelove*. This was Cook's first experience as a sailor. The voyages were restricted to the North Sea, but he learned a lot from skipper Walker. When in 1756 the Seven Years' War with France broke out, Cook, who meanwhile had risen to be a helmsman, volunteered for the Navy as an ordinary seaman.

Here he had to start again from the bottom. His mates were rough fellows, some of whom had been pressed into

James Cook

Cook's voyages

Legend:
...... Cook's First voyage 1768
----- Second voyage 1772
—— Third voyage 1776

Petropavlovsk
1779
1779
AUSTRALIA
1780
1771
Tasmania
NEW ZEALAND
1775
1773
ANTARCTICA

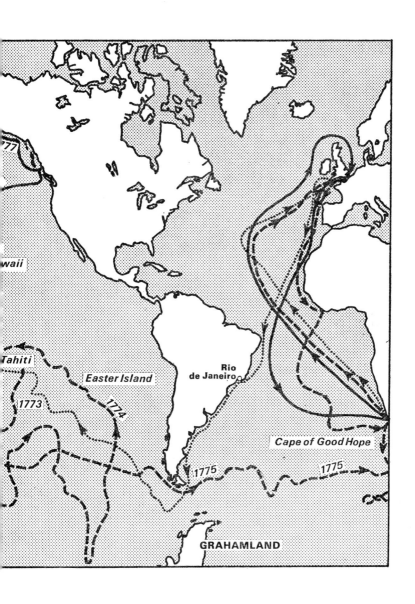

77

waii

Tahiti

1773

1774

Easter Island

Rio
de Janeiro

1775

1775

Cape of Good Hope

GRAHAMLAND

service in the Navy as a punishment. Cook's capacities were soon noted and he was promoted to boatswain. It then took several years before he got his big chance. The course of the St. Lawrence in Canada had to be charted so that the British Navy could sail up the river. James Cook was appointed to carry out this dangerous task. He set out with two assistants. At night his rowing boat crept up the rapid unknown current. The numerous rocks and shallows had to be charted and the strength of the current measured. Cook did all this almost under the very noses of the French.

The marvellous feat was accomplished. Guided by Cook, at the rudder of the leading ship, the Navy sailed up the river and safely reached Quebec. He had made his name as an explorer. Further difficult tasks followed and each time the work of this quiet man surpassed his superiors' expectation.

When therefore a leader was sought for a large-scale expedition to the Pacific, James Cook was the obvious choice. He was promoted to lieutenant in the Navy and in 1768 he set out on his first long voyage. His ship was the *Endeavour*, a converted cargo-vessel which he had chosen himself, and the crew consisted of picked men. With the exception of Cook himself, all the officers had sailed the Pacific before. A rich young scholar, Sir Joseph Banks, also took part in the voyage.

At first there were some difficulties. The sailors refused the lemon juice and the pickled cabbage, things which were strange to them, but which Cook had brought as preventatives against scurvy. Nor did they find to their taste the captain's strict demands concerning order and cleanliness.

Cook made straight for Tahiti, which had been discovered the year before by Samuel Wallis. Here the officers made astronomical observations. After a lengthy stay in the island the search for the Southern Continent began. First Cook penetrated deep into southern waters, but he found nothing. Then the ship made for New Zealand and thoroughly explored the coast, more thoroughly than had been done by Tasman a hundred and thirty years earlier. Cook established that it consisted of two islands and charted the straits between so correctly that his observations are used even now. He then sailed westwards, to Australia, and began to explore the coast of this continent. Here the *Endeavour* ran into great danger, for an enormous coral reef lies along the east coast. Again and again currents and wind threatened to drive the ship on the rocks. For a long time Cook and his men prevented this happening, but on one occasion the *Endeavour* did run aground. Fortunately they were able to repair the leak in time.

Finally Cook returned to his homeland via New Guinea and Java. Apart from various new territories, other discoveries had been made during the voyage. It had been proved that pickled cabbage and lemon juice, together with the captain's high standards of order and cleanliness, had indeed benefited the crew: for the first time on such a long voyage scurvy had claimed no victims.

As early as 1772 Cook set out for a second voyage, this time with two ships and the instruction to find the Southern Continent, come what may. On this occasion, too, some scholars, the Fosters – father and son – joined the expedition. This time Cook first made for the Cape of Good Hope and then set a southerly course. The English went so far south that their ships ended up in the icefield of Antarctica.

Creaking and cracking they made their way through the ice, threatened by icebergs and fog, until the crew's exhaustion forced Cook to leave the polar regions in order to recover their strength in the warm palm islands of the Pacific. In Tahiti Cook met old friends, and the inhabitants of the Tonga Islands also received a prolonged visit. But then Cook once more continued his search for the Southern Continent. Again his ships sailed through ice and fog, until at last the captain was convinced that the Southern Continent did not exist, or rather, could not be reached. He returned home.

The Endeavour, *in which Cook set out for his first great voyage of discovery*

By now the ship's boy of the *Freelove* had become a famous man. He had sailed the oceans and had penetrated the ice of the Antarctic. There was nothing left for him to discover in the south. But in the northern Pacific there were still unknown regions, and in 1776 Cook was put in command of an expedition for the third time. This time the question was whether a way through could be found north of America. If anyone could find the answer to this question it was he. Together with men who had accompanied him on previous voyages, the captain set course for the north.

In the course of this voyage Cook discovered the Hawaiian Islands. From there the ships sailed to the coast of Canada and began their search in the cold arctic waters. Everywhere they found themselves obstructed by the ice. Enormous ice-floes endangered the ships and severe gales made the sailors shiver in their heavy jackets. The sails were covered in ice and the ropes became so stiff that they could hardly be tied. None of the crew protested when Cook finally gave the order to return south.

They intended to recover in the Hawaiian Islands, but it was here that the expedition received the greatest possible setback . . . in a clash with a group of natives Cook was killed. James Cook, who had travelled over 100,000 km and in all his encounters with foreign peoples had always found the right word, lost his life as the result of a misunderstanding. Hawaiian priests thought Cook to be a kind of god, but when, unbeknown to him, they put him to the test, he proved to be an ordinary human being. This cost him his life.

As a result of Cook's voyages many empty spots on the map could be filled in. As far as the discovery of the oceans is concerned, this is almost the end of the story. Travellers who sailed the high seas after Cook could only make small-scale discoveries.

But in the large continents of Asia and Africa there were still many unknown regions. Most of these were to be explored in the course of the nineteenth century.

THE NINETEENTH CENTURY

America: from coast to coast

In the early nineteenth century the United States still formed only a young, just developing nation. Its territory consisted mainly of a broad strip along the Atlantic coast. Little was known about the land which lay beyond this strip. The course of the Mississippi had been known since La Salle's expedition, but the area to the west still had to be explored.

In order to get some idea of this unknown territory, the U.S. government in 1804 sent out an expedition led by two officers, the Captains Lewis and Clark. On a fine March morning they set out from a frontier village situated at the confluence of the Mississippi and the Missouri. This village, with its blockhouses and palisades was later to grow into the industrial city of St. Louis, a city as large as Liverpool. Lewis and Clark decided to follow the course of the Missouri and patiently they and their men paddled up the river, which is 4000 km. long. They passed waterfalls and rapids and looked in amazement at the incredibly large numbers of deer. The members of the expedition ate well: every day they had fresh venison, spit-roasted over their campfire.

After a few months' travelling, the wooded landscape gave way to enormous prairies, green as meadows and level as football fields. Here bison grazed and here lived the Prairie Indians. The expedition passed the winter with one of these tribes, the Mandan.

In the spring they continued on their way, still paddling

up the Missouri. As the river became narrower, the Americans saw more and more beavers which had built their dams everywhere. Finally they reached the region which is now the State of Montana, and here began the most difficult part of their journey. The travellers were forced to leave their canoes behind and to try to buy horses from the Soshones who lived there.

Lewis and Clark were hospitably received by these Indians. Lewis described it as follows in his journal:

13th August 1805
We had walked almost two miles when we met a group of around sixty warriors riding magnificent horses. I went forward, leaving my gun behind, but carrying the flag. The Indian Chief also came forward, accompanied by two others. They embraced me warmly in their own way, namely by placing their left arm across my right shoulder and slapping me on the back, meanwhile pressing their left cheek against mine and shouting something like 'a hi e, a hi e'. This means something like 'I am very happy'. Then the others approached and we slapped each other warmly on the back. We were all covered in grease and paint and I became exhausted by all these caresses. I then lit a pipe and let everyone smoke it in turn. Before the Indians did so, they sat down and took off their mocassins, as was the custom among this tribe. Later I found that this communal pipe smoking had a solemn meaning – it meant swearing friendship.

After all these expressions of friendship, the Americans soon succeeded in buying a number of horses and now the trek across the Rocky Mountains could begin. But

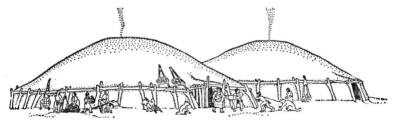

Agricultural village of the Mandan Indians

The exploration of America

here their luck ran out. Winter came early and snow and gales made the mountains almost impassable. Several of the packhorses fell into ravines and the travellers began to suffer from lack of food.

At last, after long and difficult days, the land levelled out. The Rocky Mountains had been conquered. When they reached a small river, it was decided to take to the water once more. The members of the expedition bought a number of boats from local Indians and set out. As Orellana had done long ago on the Amazon, the Americans saw the river constantly getting deeper and wider and when they finally reached the Pacific coast, the Columbia River had become a mighty stream.

Numerous other travellers were to follow in their footsteps: fur-trappers and merchants, but also farmers and cattle breeders, who were to capture the land from the Indians in heavy fighting and to give the United States their present form.

Africa: the riddle of the rivers

On 21 June 1795, the young Scottish physician Mungo Park set foot on land near the mouth of the Gambia River. He had been sent out by the African Association in London to trace the course of the Niger. Park was to be unlucky. Though his first expedition in fact took him as far as the Niger, the hostile attitude of the Mohammedan population towards the Christian traveller forced him to turn back. Robbed of all his possessions he returned to to the coast. A few years later the hardy Scot again set out. This time he succeeded in following the course of the Niger for quite a long way, but in 1805 he was drowned during a fight with natives. It was not until 1830 that the Lander brothers succeeded in completing Park's work and charting the rest of the river.

In that same period another expedition was undertaken by the Frenchman René Caillé, who travelled to the Sahara via the Sudan to find the mysterious city of Timbuktu. The accounts of Arabian travellers such as Ibn Batuta had described it as a rich and splendid commercial city. What would it be like after so many centuries? When Caillé approached Timbuktu he wrote in his journal:

I could hardly contain myself for joy. Would I see a large, prosperous city? All I saw was a number of mud huts in a large sandy plain ... The sky above it was a dusty red. It was a dreary and lonely sight.

The city, once so powerful, had fallen into decay and was now only a poverty-stricken village. Deeply disappointed Caillé returned home. When he reported his experiences in France, nobody would believe him.

Park, the Lander brothers and Caillé were the first of a stream of travellers to penetrate Africa in the course of the nineteenth century. Scholars, missionaries, merchants and men intent on conquest came from all sides. Their travels were hard and mostly on foot. They crossed sultry forests and scorched, barren plains. Native bearers carried the luggage and in each village the travellers had to barter for food and ask permission to continue. When at night they at last had some time to themselves, they had to write up their journals, to work out their notes about people, animals and plants, and to compile maps from the details they had noted in the course of the day. They worked by the light of a candle, keeping away the clouds of mosquitoes only by the dense smoke of their pipe or their cigar. Explorers often fell ill as a result of bad food or drinking water, and they suffered from malaria which slowly but surely undermined their strength. Only the very strong were able to travel in the unknown regions of Africa in this manner.

One of the chief problems which these travellers tried to solve was to establish the course of the great rivers, the Nile, the Congo and the Zambesi. Park and the Landers had found the course of the Niger, but the names of other explorers are linked with the study of the other three rivers.

Around 1850 the missionary David Livingstone succeeded in the course of several, by now famous expeditions, to establish the course of the Zambesi. On one of his travels he was attacked by a lion and seriously injured. When the pious missionary was asked later what his

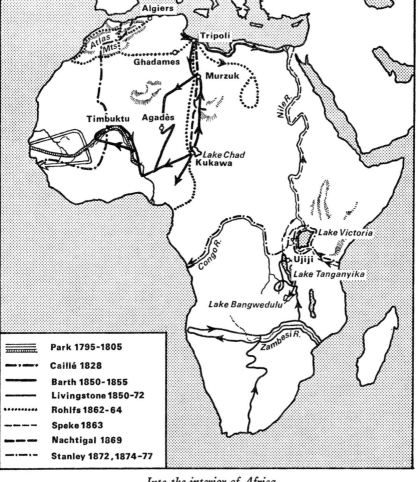

Legend:

- ══════ Park 1795-1805
- ──·─·── Caillé 1828
- ──────── Barth 1850-1855
- ──────── Livingstone 1850-72
- •••••••••• Rohlfs 1862-64
- ── ── ── Speke 1863
- ── ── ── Nachtigal 1869
- ──·──·── Stanley 1872,1874-77

Into the interior of Africa

thoughts had been at this dangerous moment, he replied:
'I wondered which part of me he would eat first.'

He was deeply moved by the misery caused in Africa by
the slave trade. He saw the devastated villages, and the
columns of prisoners being driven along, and he experienced the despair of those who were left behind. He was to
devote the rest of his life to combating this trade in
human beings. He came to the conclusion that the interior

71

Stanley finds Livingstone

of Africa had great need of European goods, which tempted many tribal chiefs to supply negroes for the slave caravans. To combat the slave trade it would be necessary to flood the interior with the coveted European wares. This would be possible only if good trade routes were available. Livingstone therefore decided to search for such routes. To his great disappointment the Zambesi proved to be unsuitable, since the numerous rapids and great waterfalls made navigation impossible.

In the course of his second large expedition, which started in 1858, he discovered Lake Nyasa. To his dismay this provided the slave traders with a new route into the interior. Worried and tired, the ageing missionary in 1866 set out on his third great journey. His purpose was twofold: he wanted to investigate how deeply the slave trade had penetrated into Central Africa, and at the same time he wanted to find the sources of the Nile.

The latter had, in fact, already been found when in 1863 John Speke reached Lake Victoria and established that it is from this lake, twice the size of Scotland, that the Nile streams northwards. Livingstone wanted to find out whether another river flowed into this lake, which would be the very origin of the Nile.

This third expedition was to be Livingstone's last. Accompanied by a constantly dwindling group of faithful negro servants, the ailing missionary travelled through swamps and forests. He discovered Lake Tanganyika and several smaller lakes, crossed numerous large and small rivers, but at last he collapsed. Illness and exhaustion prevented him from going on and he sought refuge in the little village of Ujiji on the shores of Lake Tanganyika, to recover his strength. He had been living there for some time when on November 10, 1871, his servant Susi came running into his house and exclaimed that a white man was approaching. On hearing this news, Livingstone went outside and saw a long column of bearers, led by a young man. The latter came up to the missionary and spoke the famous words:

*'Doctor Livingstone, I presume?'
'Yes,' said he, lifting his cap slightly.
'I thank God I have been permitted to see you.'

The young man who had arrived in Ujiji so unexpectedly was called Henry Morton Stanley. He was a reporter on the *New York Herald* and had been sent out by his editor to search for Livingstone. Stanley himself described how he was given the task:

In Paris I went straight to the Grand Hotel and knocked on Bennet's door.
'Come in,' someone called.
When I entered, I found Mr. Bennet in bed.
'Who are you?'
'My name is Stanley.'
'Sit down. Where do you think Livingstone is?'
'I don't know.'
'I want you to go and find him.'
'Is that so. Do you really think I'll go to Central Africa?'
'Yes. The old man may be in trouble. Take everything you may need to help him.'
'But have you thought how much such an expedition will cost?'
'Listen. You will start by taking up a thousand pounds. When you've spent it you take up a further thousand pounds, and so on. But go and find Livingstone.'

* (Transl. note: From *How I found Livingstone* by Henry Morton Stanley.)

In the course of Stanley's visit to Livingstone several trips were made to Lake Tanganyika

This is how an American journalist suddenly became an African explorer. He had no experience whatsoever in travelling in unknown territory, accompanied by bearers, but he learned surprisingly fast. With unusual speed he drove his men across plains and mountains, through forests and swamps, to the shores of Lake Tanganyika. And there, in Ujiji, he did indeed find Livingstone.

The two men stayed together for several months. Stanley replenished Livingstone's stores and returned to the coast. He was the last white man to see the old missionary.

Livingstone once more set off for the Bangweulu swamps, where he died of exhaustion on 29 April 1872.

His faithful servants decided not to bury him there, but carried his body to the coast. It took them nine months to cover the 2000 km. which separated them from the sea. From there an English warship took the explorer's remains to England where they were ceremoniously interred in Westminster Abbey.

It was Stanley who finally solved the riddle of the Nile and the Congo. The intrepid journalist-explorer led a large expedition into the interior. Among other things his bearers carried the component parts of a complete small steamboat. He started from Zanzibar in 1874 and exactly nine hundred and ninety days later the exhausted survivors of the enterprise stumbled into Cabinda, a village at the mouth of the Congo River. Stanley had literally forced his way through rocks, forests and hostile tribes.

Hundreds of bearers, and all his white companions, had perished on the way. Stanley later described his journey in two large volumes: the expedition, in the course of which Lake Victoria was charted as well as the Ruwenzori Mountains and Lake Tanganyika, and during which Stanley travelled down one river after another, until he finally reached the wide Congo. This was the journey which earned him the nickname 'Bula Matari': the man who crushes rocks.

Africa's interior had been opened up and the riddles of the rivers had been solved.

Africa: desert adventures

By the middle of the nineteenth century the Sahara was still practically unknown to Europeans. Travel in this enormous area, fourteen times the size of France, was

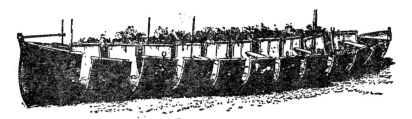

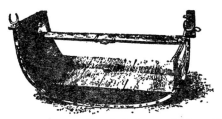

Stanley's boat, which could be dismantled

difficult. It is a thinly-populated desert, where food and especially drinking water are hard to come by. The desert tribes, Tuaregs, Tibu and Berbers, were moreover hostile towards Europeans. They regarded white men as despicable Christian dogs and tried to prevent them from penetrating the area by all possible means.

Nevertheless several brave men defied the horrors of heat, thirst and hatred to explore the Sahara. We have already mentioned the Frenchman Caillé. The men who will be discussed in this chapter were all three Germans. The first was the geographer Dr. Heinrich Barth, who travelled the Sahara and the Sudan from 1850 to 1855. From Tripoli he went south towards Agadès, where he remained for a long time. The inhabitants of the desert soon learned to value the clever scholar. He was given the name Abd-el-Kerim: Servant of God. For hours on end he conversed with Mohammedan religious scholars. His wide knowledge made him a match for them and enabled him to defend Christian ideas.

After his stay in Agadès, Barth continued on his way and reached Lake Chad. He found that this is a fresh-water lake, hardly more than five feet deep. Desert lakes are usually salt-water lakes and Barth tried to discover an explanation for this remarkable phenomenon. He supposed that the lake had an underground drainage system and this theory was confirmed by subsequent research.

Barth then visited the town of Kuka in the Sultanate of Bornu, where he lived for some years. From there he made several journeys in the surrounding areas. He was hospitably received by sultans and other dignitaries and made a thorough study of countries and peoples.

Finally he visited Timbuktu, where he ascertained that Caillé had spoken the truth, and then returned to Tripoli. His books gave Europeans some idea of the Sahara and the Sudan. Barth had made a start, and others were to continue his activities.

After Barth the most important explorer was the

German doctor Gerhard Rohlfs, who started his career as physician to the court of the Sultan of Morocco. To achieve his goal he dressed as a Moroccan, shaved his head and entered the interior in yellow slippers. From then onwards he had to behave like a Mohammedan and be constantly on his guard not to betray himself. He learned to eat with his fingers and forced himself to sit for hours on end, conversing quietly, which was a difficult task for such a restless man. In addition he had to quote suitable passages from the Koran on all sorts of occasions.

After having worked in Morocco for a year, he was the first white man to go south into the Atlas Mountains. Here he nearly lost his life. He was shot at in his sleep by brigands and was hit in the left arm. As he tried to jump up to seize his pistol, his right arm was seriously injured by a sword. He fainted as a result of his wounds, and the brigands left him for dead among the rocks. There he lay for three days until he was found by Moroccan shepherds, who took the badly injured man to their village. They nursed Rohlfs with the greatest care until, after several weeks' rest, he was able to return to the coast.

In 1864 Rohlfs set out again. This time his goal was Timbuktu, which he wanted to reach by going south from Algiers. Entirely alone, he succeeded in crossing the Atlas Mountains and reaching the oasis of Tafilelt. The inhabitants had great admiration for 'Mustafa', as Rohlfs called himself. The Atlas Mountains were dangerous and difficult to cross. They themselves only went there in large groups. Although Rohlfs had now overcome the first obstacle, he was still separated from Timbuktu by the endless plains of the Sahara. Travelling with caravans, the brave doctor penetrated far south, but he never reached his goal. Wars were raging in the area of Timbuktu, and the caravans did not venture into the region. He therefore decided to go east. Some of the difficulties which the traveller had to overcome on his journey to Ghadames are described in the following passage from his journal:

Before us lay the desolate emptiness of the Sahara: a *sserir* – a plain strewn with multi-coloured grit hardly larger than hazelnuts. There was no point where the tired eye could rest. It was one single, blinding carpet of stone – and endlessly large mozaic. No plant, no animal, no tree, no shrub was visible. Suddenly a lake shimmers in the cloudless sky and it seems as if the water ripples in a slight breeze – and then it disappears again. It is a *fata morgana* – a vision, a mirage.

After a hard journey through the sand dunes of Libya, he reached the port of Tripoli, where honour and glory awaited him. He had become a famous man and the king of Prussia asked him to take a number of gifts to the Sultan of Bornu, whose guest Barth had been for so long some years earlier. But Rohlf did not relish this task, however honourable. He thought it too tame and unexciting. He therefore searched for a deputy and found one in the person of another German physician, Gustav Nachtigal, who lived in Tripoli for the sake of his health. Although Nachtigal had no experience whatever of desert travel, he accepted the task, and thus began one of the most thrilling expeditions in the entire history of the discovery of the Sahara.

As a guide he took Mohammed el-Gatrun, who had earlier accompanied both Barth and Rohlfs. Mohammed was an elderly man, but he was a most reliable guide and caravan leader. He was to be young Nachtigal's indispensable support and shield. They set out early in 1869. The first part of the journey, from Tripoli to Murzuq, went well. But in this oasis the travellers met with a disagreeable delay: the next caravan to the south would not leave for at least six months. The doctor did not like the idea of waiting in Murzuq, where malaria, heat, dust and boredom were all he could expect. He therefore decided to use the interval for a visit to the Mountains of Tibesti, where the Tibu lived. Everyone advised him against it. The Tibu were notorious brigands and it was thought impossible that Nachtigal would survive the adventure. The faithful Mohammed, too, repeatedly pointed out the great dangers

Desert warrior as encountered by Nachtigal

attached to such an expedition. But when Nachtigal suggested that he should stay in Murzuq to guard the gifts for the Sultan of Bornu, he gave his master a dignified reply, so dignified, that Nachtigal recorded it in his journal:

> I have promised your friends in Tripoli to take you safely to Bornu, just as I guided your brothers, Barth and Rohlfs there. With God's help we shall reach this goal together. Until then I shall not desert you, and if you are to perish among the treacherous Tibu, I shall share your fate.

Thus Gustav Nachtigal and Mohammed el-Gatrun set out for the mountain area of the Tibu in June 1869. Their guide was a Tibu, Kokomi, who said he was a nobleman in his own country. The party travelled eastwards through the lonely desert. After four weeks of heat, thirst and endless days' marches, they reached the mountains of Tibesti and the first white man entered the notorious land of the Tibu. After some days they met a group of warriors who demanded large ransoms before they were allowed to continue. In exchange for the goods received, the chief warrior, Arami, took the travellers under his protection. But little good was in store for them in Bardai, the main Tibu village. The inhabitants surrounded them threateningly and Arami had difficulty in taking them to his house. Here they were safe – but they were virtually prisoners. They remained there for several weeks until at last the Tibu managed one night to take them outside the village. Robbed of practically all their possessions, the travellers were abandoned on the plateau. A grim journey to the safety of Murzuq, 800 km. away, awaited them. They reached the town at last, more dead than alive. Everyone was amazed that they had got out of the clutches of the Tibu at all.

A few months later, Nachtigal and his men joined a large caravan which was travelling south, and in the summer of 1870 the Prussian king's gifts were handed over to the Sultan of Bornu.

The expeditions of Barth, Rohlfs and Nachtigal had opened up the great routes through the Sahara to Europeans. Much was still to be explored, but as had been the case after Cook's voyages, later travellers would be able to build on the foundations laid by these pioneers.

Asia : The secret of the Forbidden City

At the time of Livingstone's and Barth's expeditions in Africa, two monks were travelling through China. They were Father Huc and Father Gabet and their objective was the 'forbidden' Holy City of Lhasa in Tibet. This was the centre of the Buddhist world, where the Dalai Lama, the high priest and ruler, lived in an enormous monastery. Neither the Chinese nor the Tibetans liked foreigners travelling through their country and Huc and Gabet therefore disguised themselves as lamas, or Tibetan

Tibetan monk

monks. This was a dangerous thing to do, for if their
disguise were to be discovered, it might cost them their
lives. Nevertheless Huc and his companion donned the
yellow habits, secured with five gilt buttons, and the red
girdles. They wrapped themselves in red mantles with
dark velvet collars and put on red-plumed yellow hats.
Their journey first led through densely populated regions
of China. The further west they travelled, the more
inhospitable the countryside became and the two monks
had to cross mountains, steppes and deserts. In the beginning they spent the nights in dirty inns, where they had to
bargain over the bill. Later they joined caravans. These
were hard days, for the pack-animals were loaded in the
early hours and did not halt until late in the afternoon.

They had their first real rest in the lamasery of Kunbum,
close to the Tibetan border, where the travellers knocked
on the door late one night. The monks immediately put a
room at their disposal and provided a late evening meal.
Huc described it as follows:

> They brought tea with milk and a large dish of mutton, fresh
> butter and some rolls. Our hearts were filled with joy. That
> night, when we were alone, we could not sleep. We meditated

on the strange situation in which we found ourselves. It was hardly believable. Here we were in the unknown land of Amdo, in the famous lamasery of Kunbum.

Soon Huc and Gabet were entirely at home in the buddhist monastery. They had long discussions on religion with the lamas and even fitted up their own little chapel. But the superior of the monastery thought this was going too far and the two foreigners were requested to leave. After some months the enterprising monks therefore continued on their way. In the company of a number of lamas they travelled to the near-by lake of Koko Nor. Here they joined a large caravan which was on its way to Lhasa. The company consisted of over two thousand people and they used horses, camels and yaks. The latter are a kind of long-haired oxen which in the highlands of Tibet are used as pack-animals and mounts. After long days' marches through the savage mountain region, this group reached the holy city of Lhasa on 9 January 1846.

After only a short stay in the city, Huc and Gabet were sent back, to their great disappointment. Nevertheless the two travellers supplied a great deal of information about the interior of Asia. Spurred on by their reports, more and more brave men were to explore these regions. Russians such as Nikolai Przhewalsky, Indians like Pandit Krishna (whose journey was so secret that he was referred to in

Llasa, with the Potala, the Dalai Lama's palace

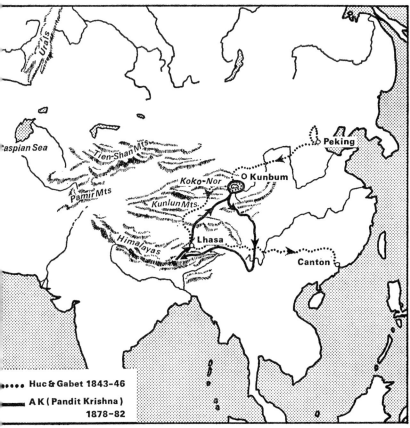

Huc & Gabet 1843–46

AK (Pandit Krishna)
1878–82

Discoveries in China and Tibet

the documents of his employers only as 'A-K') and many others. The most famous of them all was the Swede Sven Hedin who, between 1890 and 1935, undertook seven great expeditions, visiting and charting the entire region between the Himalayas and the Tien Shan Mountains.

THE TWENTIETH CENTURY

We have almost come to the end of the history of voyages of discovery.

All the inhabited regions of the world were known by now. Only the two polar regions had as yet withstood man's assaults. But this too was soon to change, for explorers were to penetrate deeper and deeper into both arctic regions.

The conquest of the North Pole

Several travellers seeking routes through the frozen polar regions have already been mentioned: Cartier, Frobisher, Davis, Barents, Heemskerck. They were all forced to turn back without achieving their objectives. In the nineteenth century, too, it proved to be impossible to surmount the obstacles. Several brave men lost their lives. On one occasion an entire expedition, consisting of two ships carrying a hundred and twenty-nine men under the command of Sir John Franklin, disappeared in Arctic waters. But again and again courageous explorers hoped to succeed where others had failed.

One famous voyage was that of Fridtjof Nansen, a Norwegian scholar who set out for the arctic in 1893 in a specially built, very strong ship, the *Fram*. When he reached the polar sea he allowed the *Fram* to become immobilised in the ice, hoping that the current would take the ice, and with it his ship, to the North Pole. Although the *Fram* came fairly close to the Pole, Nansen did not reach his objective. With a single companion, called Johanssen he therefore left the ship and attempted to cover the rest

Fridtjof Nansen   *Robert Peary*

of the way in sledges drawn by dogs. Again he was unsuccessful. After a hard winter in the polar region the two men finally managed to get back to the inhabited world, together with the *Fram*, which had freed itself and returned to Norway after having been caught in the ice for nearly a thousand days. Nowadays the *Fram* stands in a museum in Oslo and every year numerous visitors are amazed to think that such a small ship could have made such a voyage.

It was the American naval officer Robert Peary who in 1909 at last reached the North Pole. Peary's expedition left on 28 February. With his servant Henson and four Eskimos he set off for the north in a number of sledges drawn by huskies. In several places snow huts were built and provisions stored. They were therefore travelling light when in the morning of 2 April they prepared themselves for the final stretch. They travelled to the most northerly point on earth in four days of fast travel, covering 50 km. a day. These last few days were the hardest. Peary's journal describes them as follows:

The biting cold would have been impossible to face by anyone not fortified by an inflexible purpose. The bitter wind burned our faces so that they cracked and long after we got into camp each day they pained so that we could hardly go to sleep. The Eskimos complained much, which I had never known them to do before.

On reaching the Pole, he ceremoniously planted the American flag in the ice. The men made a number of observations and then began the walk back. The provisions left behind stood them in good stead. In fast tempo the sledges raced from one post to another, and within three weeks they reached their point of departure.

Peary's expedition had proved two things: firstly, that travelling with dog-sledges was a practical proposition, and secondly, that leaving provisions at various points made a speedy return possible.

Now only the South Pole remained.

The 'Fram'

The race for the South Pole

On several occasions able captains had tried to penetrate the region of the South Pole. James Cook, in particular, had made serious attempts. But not until the nineteenth century was Antarctica to be reached.

In 1820 a group of American seal-hunters had come down the coast of South America to the seas around Cape Horn. As their catch was disappointing, one of the small ships, commanded by Nat Palmer, was sent out on reconnaissance. With difficulty the ship, the *Nero*, cruised among the ice-floes in the stormy waters, until one grey November morning Palmer saw land in the distance – a coast rising sheer from the sea. He had discovered the Southern Continent, sought for so long and so laboriously. The last riddle of the earth was about to be solved, but Palmer was disappointed. There were no seals. . . .

A few weeks later a Russian expedition led by Von Bellingshausen also reached the antarctic region. The Russians happened to encounter Palmer and when Von Bellingshausen heard about his discovery, he decided to call the land which the American had found Palmer Land.

Robert Scott

Roald Amundsen

The exploration of the new continent could now begin, but it was not until the end of the century that the first great expeditions were organised. In 1911 two groups of men set out for the South Pole by different routes. One of these was led by the Norwegian explorer Roald Amundsen. The necessary supplies were carried in dog-sledges. The other group was under the leadership of the experienced Englishman Robert Scott. He had no dogs, but used ponies instead, which, however, all died on the way. Amundsen reached the South Pole on 14 December 1911 after a successful journey. Scott and his men arrived exactly a month later and found to their amazement and their great disappointment that someone else had beaten them to it. The Norwegian flag was fluttering proudly in the wind. The British could only plant their own beside it. Dejectedly they set out on the return journey. The road to the Pole had been hard, but the way back was to be even harder. They were held up repeatedly by severe weather. Some members of the group died of cold and exhaustion, until finally only three men were left – Scott and two others. Their food supply was nearly exhausted. They tried desperately to reach the food depot they had set up on their way out, until an incredibly heavy snow-storm, which raged for nine days on end, forced them to halt. Their fate was sealed. They perished of hunger and cold a mere 20 km from safety. . . .

The glacier of horror

It needed many more expeditions to learn something about Antarctica, which is almost the size of Europe. Numerous brave men devoted their best efforts to this task. Among the most famous of these was the Australian Douglas Mawson.

In 1912 he made his incredible journey across Wilkes Land, the area immediately south of Australia. With two others he left during the month of November, which is summer in Antarctica. One of his companions was a military man called Ninnis, the other was a very tall Swiss named Mertz. The first part of the journey went smoothly. The dogs drew the sledges with ease and the men were confident that their expedition would be successful. The difficulties began when they reached the glacier. The ice was criss-crossed by numerous, enor-mously deep crevasses (splits in the ice), made practically invisible by a thin layer of snow. The expedition was in constant danger of falling down one of these crevasses.

They proceeded very slowly, testing all the time to see whether the snow-layer would hold them. To minimise the risk they walked at some distance from each other. The robust Mertz went first with a lightweight sledge. Next came Mawson, also with a light sledge, and finally Ninnis with the heavy luggage sledge. For some time all went well, but on 14 December misfortune struck. While Mertz and Mawson cautiously made their way across a deep crevasse, Ninnis waited, to follow if all was well. When Mertz looked back he did not see Ninnis. His sledge had disappeared as well. Quickly the two men went back. Where Ninnis had stood there was an enormous hole in the snow. An unfathomably deep crevasse had swallowed the small man. Numb with despair his friends stood by the icy grave. Ninnis was dead and all the stores were lost. What were they to do? The base camp, where the other members of the expedition had remained, was nearly five hundred kilometres away. The two survivors would be able to complete the return journey only by using the little food they had extremely sparingly. Grimly they started on the long trek. They began to be tormented by hunger. The few remaining dogs were eaten one by one, until at last the men had to pull the sledges themselves. Mertz in particular was in a bad state. Being so large he needed a great deal of food – the small rations hit him very hard. The men advanced more and more slowly. At last Mertz had to give up. During an extra rest day he fell asleep in his sleeping-bag never to awake. Now Mawson was alone. He was 144 km from the base camp, with only a few pounds of food and badly injured feet.

He started off without hope, driven only by his iron will. For five, six days things went fairly well, but then the worst weather he had ever experienced broke out. . . . Fighting against the biting wind, crawling across the iron-hard ice, he went on. On one occasion he fell into a deep crevasse. The sledge he was pulling miraculously caught on a ridge. When Mawson dared to open his eyes

Douglas Mawson

he was hanging from a thin rope above a crevasse so deep that he could not see the bottom. By exerting all his strength he succeeded in pulling himself up by the rope. Exhausted, he got into his sleeping-bag to sleep for a while. Then he continued on his desperate journey until something large loomed up in the snowstorm. Mawson stumbled towards it, praying to God that it would mean rescue. . . . He was in luck. It proved to be a heap of snow erected by the men of the base camp to serve as a beacon for Mawson's expedition. What was even more important: there was a small store of food. With renewed strength he went on his way again. Only 37 more kilometres. After a few more days he reached a cave, where more food had been stored. Then began the last few kilometres. On 8 February 1913, the exhausted Mawson stumbled into the base camp.

Others, too, have devoted their best efforts to the exploration of the South Pole. The expeditions of the Englishman Shackleton and the American Admiral Byrd have become famous. The latter was the first to make use of aeroplanes and of tractors to clear a way through the waste land. This made it possible to explore several areas which were otherwise impassable. The discoveries in the Antarctic are by no means at an end and further information is constantly being gathered.

SUMMARY OF IMPORTANT DATES

2000 B.C.	Heno's voyage to the Land of Punt
1400 B.C.	Mycenaean conquest of Crete
1200 B.C.	Sack of Troy
600 B.C.	The Phoenicians sail round Africa
500 B.C.	Hanno the Carthaginian reaches Cameroon
350 B.C.	Pytheas of Massilia visits England and Scandinavia
356–323 B.C.	Alexander the Great
30 B.C.–300 A.D.	Romans sail the Indian Ocean
476	Fall of the Western Roman Empire
750	Irish monks reach Iceland
870	Vikings in Iceland
1000	Vikings reach the coast of America
1250	Carpini's journey to the Mongolian court
1271–1295	Marco Polo's travels in Asia
1420–1460	Dom Enrique sails along the coast of Africa
1460	The Portuguese reach Sierra Leone
1487	Bartholomew Diaz reaches the Cape of Good Hope
1492	Columbus discovers America
1497	Vasco da Gama reaches India
1510–1550	The Conquistadores in Southern and Central America

1519–1521	Magellan's voyage round the world
1595	Heemskerck and Barents in Nova Zembla
1597	De Houtman and Keyser's return from Java
1602	Foundation of the United East India Company
1642	Tasman's vain search for the Southern Continent
1680	La Salle's voyage down the Mississippi
1722	Roggeveen discovers Easter Island and the Samoa Islands
1768–1779	Cook's three voyages to the Pacific
1800–1830	Park, the Lander brothers and Caillé explore the River Niger in Africa
1805	Lewis and Clark reach the west coast of the U.S.
1850–1872	Livingstone's travels in South and East Africa
1871	Stanley finds Livingstone
1870–1890	Stanley's travels in Africa
1850–1875	Barth, Rohlfs and Nachtigal explore the Sahara
1845	Huc reaches Lhasa, the 'forbidden city' in Tibet
1893	Nansen's expedition in the Arctic
1909	Peary reaches the North Pole
1911	Amundsen reaches the South Pole, followed by Scott

INDEX